Wendy Orr • Lauren Stringer

the Princess
and her
Panther

Beach Lane Books • New York London Toronto Sydney

One afternoon . . .

For James and Susan,
and George and Sally —W. O.

For Allyn, who loves great endings and brave beginnings,
and for Matthew, Ruby, and Cooper —L. S.

 BEACH LANE BOOKS
An imprint of Simon & Schuster Children's Publishing Division
1230 Avenue of the Americas, New York, New York 10020
Text copyright © 2010 by Wendy Orr
Illustrations copyright © 2010 by Lauren Stringer
All rights reserved, including the right of reproduction in whole or in part in any form.
BEACH LANE BOOKS is a trademark of Simon & Schuster, Inc.
For information about special discounts for bulk purchases, please contact Simon & Schuster
Special Sales at 1-866-506-1949 or business@simonandschuster.com.
The Simon & Schuster Speakers Bureau can bring authors to your live event. For more
information or to book an event, contact the Simon & Schuster Speakers Bureau
at 1-866-248-3049 or visit our website at www.simonspeakers.com.
Book design by Lauren Rille
The text for this book is set in Artcraft.
The illustrations for this book are rendered in acrylic paint
on gessoed 140 lb. Arches watercolor paper.
Manufactured in China
0410 SCP
First Edition
10 9 8 7 6 5 4 3 2 1
Library of Congress Cataloging-in-Publication Data
Orr, Wendy, 1953-
The princess and her panther / Wendy Orr ; illustrated by Lauren Stringer.—1st ed.
p. cm.
Summary: A brave princess and a panther who tries to be brave cross the desert together
and settle into a red silk tent, in which they listen to "leaf-snakes," an "owl-witch,"
and other frightening creatures until the princess frightens them away.
ISBN 978-1-4169-9780-1 (hardcover)
[1. Princesses—Fiction. 2. Panthers—Fiction. 3. Camping—Fiction. 4. Sisters—Fiction.
5. Fear of the dark—Fiction.] I. Stringer, Lauren, ill. II. Title.
PZ7.O746Pri 2010
[E]—dc22
2009034359

a princess and her panther crossed the desert sand.
The princess was brave, and the panther tried to be.

The panther drank from the waters of a wide blue lake,
while under a tree in the dark, deep woods,
the princess pitched her red silk tent.

The princess and her panther
watched the clouds turn to gold.
The princess was brave,
and the panther tried to be.

The sky grew purple,
and the world turned black—

and as far as they could see,
there was nothing but night.

The princess was brave,
and the panther tried to be.

The princess lit a lantern so its light shone bright

into the shadows of the red silk tent.

Then the light grew small and was swallowed by the night.

The princess was brave,
and the panther tried to be.

Then they heard

a soft, slow shivering, a *hiss-siss* slippering

of leaf-snakes slithering across their tent in the night.

The princess was brave, and the panther tried to be.

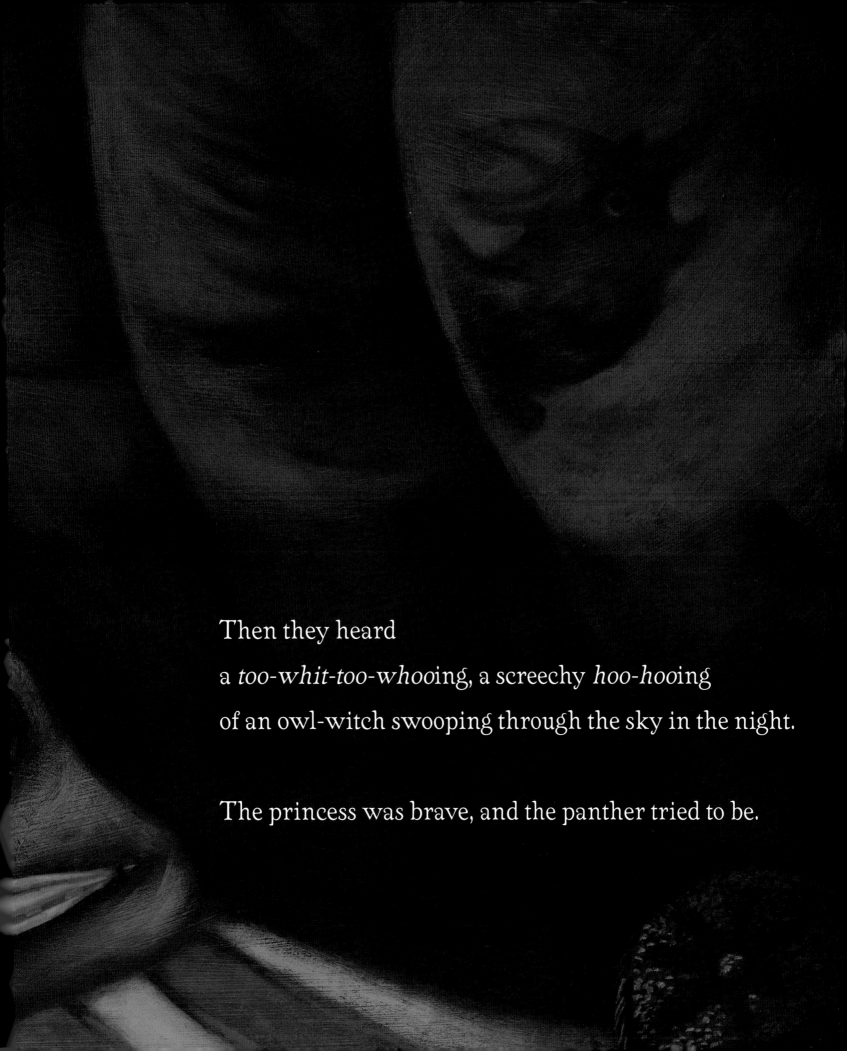

Then they heard

a *too-whit-too-whoo*ing, a screechy *hoo-hoo*ing

of an owl-witch swooping through the sky in the night.

The princess was brave, and the panther tried to be.

Then they heard

a deep, throaty moaning, a croakety groaning

of a frog-monster roaming through the lake in the night.

The princess tried to be brave,

and the panther tried to try.

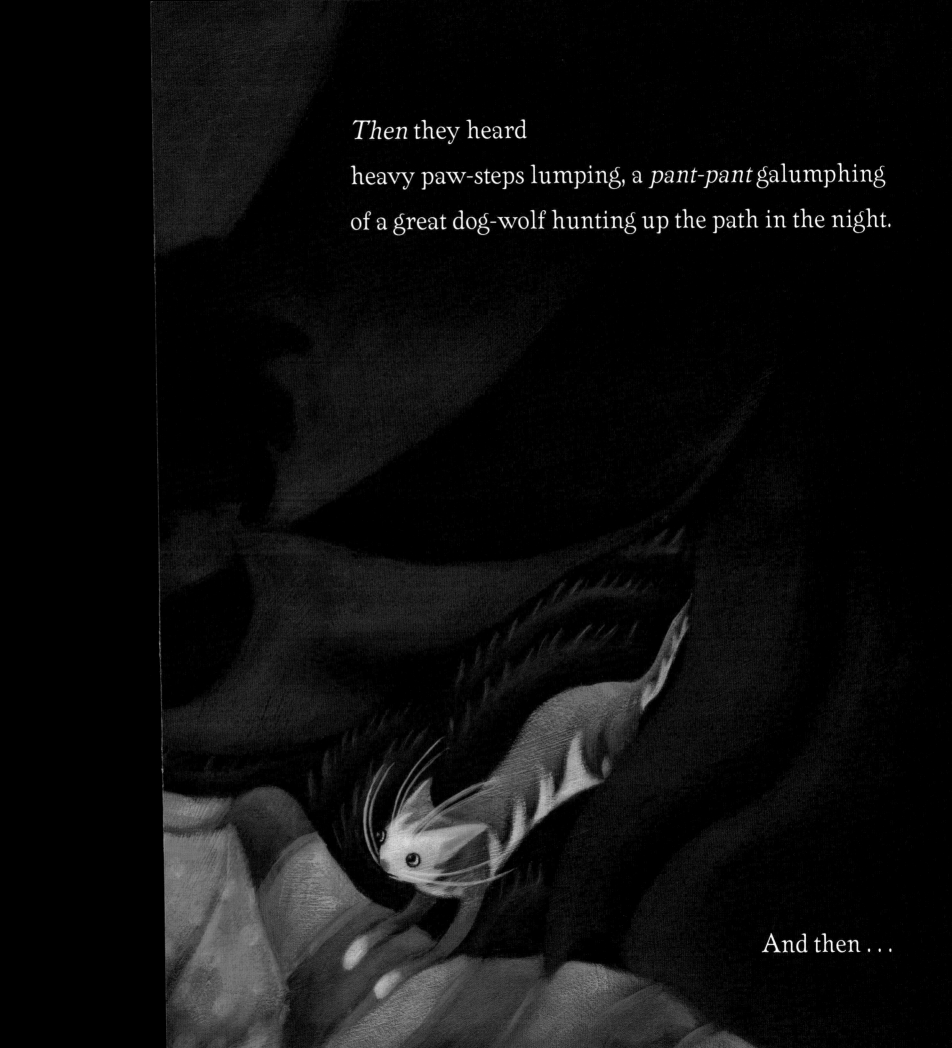

Then they heard
heavy paw-steps lumping, a *pant-pant* galumphing
of a great dog-wolf hunting up the path in the night.

And then . . .

the princess was brave,

and the panther was too.

"Enough is enough!"

And just like that . . .

the wolf ran away with a surprised sort of bark,
and the monster and the witch and the slithery snakes
vanished from the dark.

Then the princess and her panther
turned back to their tent.

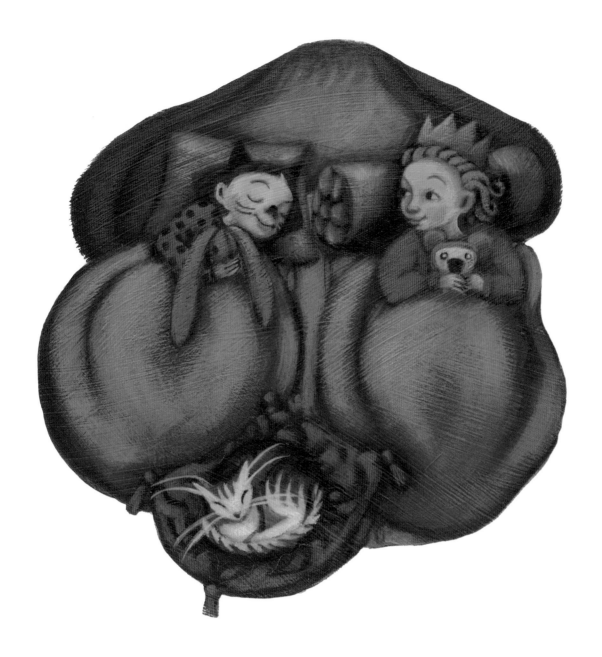

The princess said good night, the panther closed her eyes,
and the full moon smiled as it shone its soft light
on two sisters sleeping, in their tent . . .

one night.